What do the grown-ups do?

Fiona the Doctor

"To say that I was totally enamoured by the 'What do' series is something of an understatement. I always feel that the ultimate test lies in how one's own children treat such reading materials. When I asked them, if they were enjoying the books, they were unequivocal in their praise of them."
Pocketful of Rye.

"An informative and fun way to introduce your children to the world of living."
Gordon Buchanan, Wildlife Filmmaker.

"Really detailed and informative books, which contain exactly the questions that intelligent children ask, and adults are often unable to answer. There is fun, humour and a wonderful sense of place too."
Dr Ken Greig, Rector, Hutchesons' Grammar School.

"As an educator in the US there is more and more stress placed upon children being able to access non-fiction writing. Within her books, Mairi McLellan has done something many children's authors are unable to do: she has created non-fiction books that are compelling and highly readable. May all of children's non-fiction literature begin to engage students as McLellan's books do. If this is a new trend in children's books, teachers across the US would be so grateful."
Marlene Moyer, 5th and 6th Grade Teacher, Nevada, USA.

"What a refreshing an innovative way of introducing children to career possibilities in later life. A delightful series of books which gently guides younger children through the adult world of work. The accompanying photos of the main characters bring the lives of Joe the Fisherman, Fiona the Doctor and Papa the Stockfarmer to life."
Louise Webster, Broadcaster.

What do the grown-ups do?

Fiona the Doctor

Mairi McLellan

Matador
9 Priory Business Park
Kibworth Beauchamp
Leicestershire LE8 0RX, UK
Tel: (+44) 116 279 2299
Fax: (+44) 116 279 2277
Email: books@troubador.co.uk
Web: www.troubador.co.uk/matador

ISBN: 978 1783065 257

Editor: Eleanor MacCannell

British Library Cataloguing in Publication Data.
A catalogue record for this book is available from the British Library.

Matador is an imprint of Troubador Publishing Ltd

www.kidseducationalbooks.com

What do the grown-ups do?

Dear Reader,

What do the grown-ups do? is a series of books designed to educate children about the workplace using chatty, light-hearted stories, written through the eyes of the children.

The aim is to offer the children an insight into adult working life, to stimulate their thinking and to help motivate them to learn more about the jobs that interest them. Perhaps by introducing these concepts early, we can broaden their ideas for the future, as well as increase their awareness of the world around them. It's just a start, and at this age, although the message is serious, it is designed to be fun.

For younger children who will be doing a combination of reading and being read to, this series will be reasonably challenging. I have deliberately tried not to over-simplify them too much in order to maintain reality, whilst keeping the tone chatty and informal.

The books can be read in any order but they are probably best starting from the beginning. The order of the series can be found at the back of this book. Many more will be coming soon so please check the website for updates: **www.kidseducationalbooks.com**.

I hope you enjoy them.

Happy reading!

Mairi

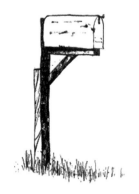

A note of thanks to my friend and sister-in-law, Fiona; for her time on the book, her time as our family doc and for all the good times biking, windsurfing, skiing and generally hanging out. Ace.

Life by the sea in Badaneel

It was summer in the Northwest Highland village of Badaneel, home to the Mackenzie girls, Ava, Skye and Gracie. Surrounded by wide sandy beaches, wooded glens and tall mountains, there was always an adventure to be had in Badaneel, but never more so than in summer!

The beaches around Badaneel.

Skye doughnuting!

Summer meant playing in the sea and, if it was calm, that meant doughnuting! The twins, Ava and Skye, and their sister, Gracie, had invited

 1

friends round to play in the doughnut. After brief instruction, they climbed over the dinghy, sat down in the doughnut, held onto the handles and were off and away! The excited screams from the children could be heard across the bay!

Skye and Gracie hold on tight.

Ava has the loudest scream!

Zooming across the bay.

To instruct the driver to go faster, the children had to point into the air. Everyone wanted to go at maximum speed! It was immensely good fun!

At the end of doughnuting, the girls went for a quick splash, jumping forwards and backwards into the sea. They could have carried on for hours, but there were many jobs that needed doing in the garden and it was time to get changed.

Skye and Ava see who can jump the furthest.

Gracie does not want to go and get changed! She wants to stay and play.

Jobs

The girls spent a lot of time playing but they also had jobs to do. It had been a really fun morning and now they were ready to help with the jobs around the house. Today it was weeding in the garden. With the big purple bucket at the ready, they got on with pulling the weeds from the paths.

Ava and Gracie working.

Gracie and Skye load the bucket with weeds.

Their parents said that it was important to work hard in life, as it gives you a sense of achievement. Importantly, it also gives you a roof over your head and money to buy things like doughnuts and dinghies, or whatever else might take your fancy. The girls were generally good workers and they knew that the faster they worked, the quicker they finished!

With everyone working together, they would soon be back to playtime! After about an hour, the girls were getting rather fed up and, as luck would have it, Auntie Fiona arrived to say hello. This only meant one thing: a tea break! Delighted at the prospect, the girls went inside. Mother was making tea in the kitchen, chatting to Auntie Fiona. She was explaining that the girls had been investigating grown-up jobs.

Skye interrupted, "Excuse me, Mama, but Auntie Fee is a doctor. Can we ask her about a doctor's job?"

"I think that's a great idea," said Mother, "as long as Auntie Fiona is not too tired after her cycle."

Fiona smiled over to Skye. "I'd be delighted to chat to you about what doctors do. What would you like to know?"

Fiona the Doctor

Auntie Fiona, or Auntie Fee as the Mackenzie girls called her, was cousin Molly's mother and she had just completed a 90km race on her bike.

Fiona was the local doctor and she was always up to some activity. She was covered in mud from her race and didn't even look tired!

Quickly, she dashed upstairs to have a shower and change into the work clothes she had brought with her, before coming back down to chat to the Mackenzie girls.

Fiona the doctor.

"What do doctors do, Auntie Fee?" asked Skye.

"Well," said Fiona, "There are lots of different types of doctors and I am called a GP, or General Practitioner. When anyone in the village is feeling unwell, they come to see their GP, or 'family doctor' as we are also known.

"Family doctors are typically the first point of contact for people when they feel ill or have injured themselves. We are trained in a wide variety of different areas, which means that we know about lots of different illnesses, but we are generally not specialists in any of them.

"Part of our job is to *diagnose* the illness. This means that we need to find out what the problem is and decide whether we can help the patient, or whether they need to go to see a specialist who knows more about a specific problem.

"Specialists are people who have spent a long time learning about one area. For example, there are knee specialists, heart specialists, lung specialists, eye specialists and so on," she explained.

"In addition to diagnosing and treating people, it is also part of our job to help educate them on how to stay healthy," she said.

"How do people stay healthy?" asked Gracie.

"The best way to keep healthy is to do plenty of exercise and eat the right kind of food. Any exercise, such as swimming, running, walking and cycling, is good for your health.

"If you combine this with eating healthy food, including plenty of fruit and vegetables, you will have a much greater chance of staying in good health. Did you know that exercise has also been proven to make you happy?" asked Fiona, smiling. The girls laughed.

"How does exercise make you happy?" asked Ava, very confused.

"Exercise releases what we call *endorphins,* which are 'happy hormones' in your brain, believed to improve your mood and increase your energy.

"It is really important to exercise regularly, preferably every day. Children between the ages of five to eighteen years should be doing at least an hour of exercise every day. You three won't have any problem with that, as you are always running around!" she laughed.

Fiona cycling.

"Is that why you exercise, Auntie Fee?" asked Gracie.

Fiona laughed. "Yes, I exercise because it gives me more energy. It also helps to strengthen the muscles in your body, including your heart. Your heart is a muscle, so if it is kept exercised, it is more healthy!"

"How can you tell if people are healthy?" asked Ava.

"Most patients let us know if there is something wrong with them, so my first job as a doctor is to listen carefully to my patient," said Fiona.

"Depending on what they have told me, I then check different parts of their body to see if there is anything wrong. Every doctor has their own doctor's bag with special tools that help us understand a patient's health. Once I have done some simple tests, I then decide whether to treat the patient myself, or refer them to a specialist," she explained.

"Why don't we have a look at what's inside the bag here at the house, and then we can head down to the doctor's surgery and have a look around?" said Fiona.

The Mackenzie girls nodded. This was going to be a full investigation into the workplace!

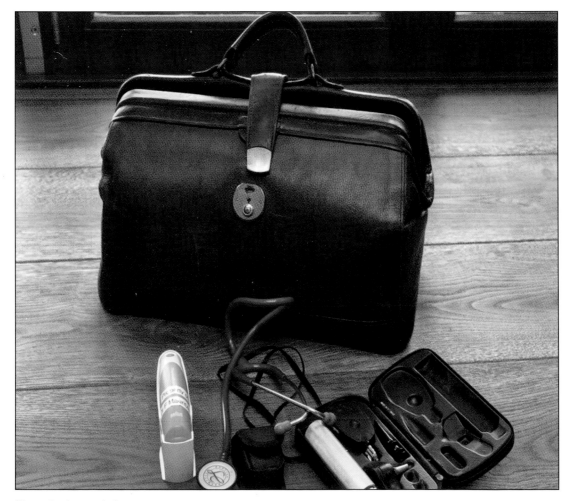

Fiona's doctor's bag.

 9

"Here we have some of the equipment that we use to help us find out, or diagnose, the patient's problem," said Fiona. "Doctors tend to use very long and complicated words to describe tools and illnesses. Don't be put off by them! Once you learn what they mean, it's much easier to understand," she smiled.

"This is a **stethoscope** [STETH-o-scope]," she said. "The stethoscope is used to listen to sounds inside the body. It has two pieces that I put in my ears, like headphones. It also has a round disc that we put on your chest. With the stethoscope, I can listen to your heart, lungs and bowels. It's very clever!

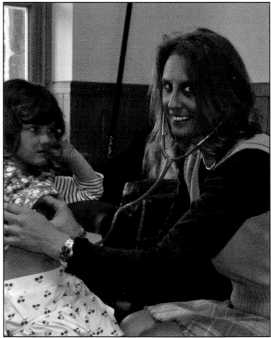

Skye and Gracie are rather unsure about the stethoscope!

"Next we have a **thermometer** [ther-MOM-et-er]. This measures body temperature and is a good way of telling us how ill a patient is. When patients are ill with an infection, they can be too hot. This particular one is an electronic thermometer that can be used to measure the body temperature through the ear. It's so quick that we have a temperature reading in only two seconds!" said Fiona.

Ava gets her temperature checked with the thermometer and sees the result.

"In some countries, they check the temperature of little children by sticking the thermometer in their bottom, but I think you might prefer the ear!" laughed Fiona. The girls laughed too. They were highly amused by any jokes about bottoms, and generally found even the mention of a bottom extremely funny. Fiona smiled. "Okay, now we'll move onto the **otoscope [OT-o-scope]**," she said.

Gracie gets her ears checked with the otoscope.

"The otoscope is an instrument used to examine the ears. Inside the ears there are things called the *ear canal* and *eardrum,* and we use the otoscope to check whether your ears are working properly," explained Fiona.

"We are looking for any signs of disease that might relate to the patient's symptoms. For example, if a patient has a sore ear, we might see redness or slight swelling. If a patient has an itchy ear, we might look for dry, flaky skin, which might be eczema related. If the patient can't hear well, the ear may be blocked with wax, or even have something stuck in it, like a rubber from the end of a pencil!"

"How do you remember all the long words?" asked Gracie.

"As with any job, you just get used to it. The more you practise, the easier it becomes, like anything you do in life," she smiled. "So, we've seen the stethoscope to check heart, lungs and bowels; the thermometer to check the

The pulse oximeter.

temperature and the otoscope to check the ears." She showed them a few other tools before moving onto a funny little gadget that clipped onto the finger.

"One of the most common problems we see are heart problems," said Fiona. "If we want to check the heart properly, the two main ways of doing this are to check the *blood pressure* and check the *pulse*.

"The pulse is a measurement of the number of beats made by the heart. To measure this we use a **pulse oximeter** [ox-IM-eter], which counts the actual number of heartbeats per minute as well as oxygen saturation, which is the amount of oxygen in your blood. We pop the oximeter onto the finger to count the beats," she said.

Gracie gets her pulse checked with the pulse oximeter.

"A normal pulse rate changes depending on the age of a person. Normal heartbeats, for example, would be:

- 100 to 160 beats every minute for babies until one year old.

- 60 to 140 for children from one to ten years old.

- 60 to 100 for children from ten years old to adulthood.

- 40 to 60 for athletes, or people who are very fit.

"Gracie, your pulse is 107, which is just right for your age!" said Fiona, smiling.

She continued pointing out items in her bag. "We're nearly there! I know it seems rather a lot to learn, but you will find it useful when you are older," she said.

Once they had finished raking through the bag, investigating all the contents, Fiona suggested they drive over to the surgery. They had been in the surgery before but they had never been able to explore properly. It was all very exciting. Inside, everything was very clean and organised.

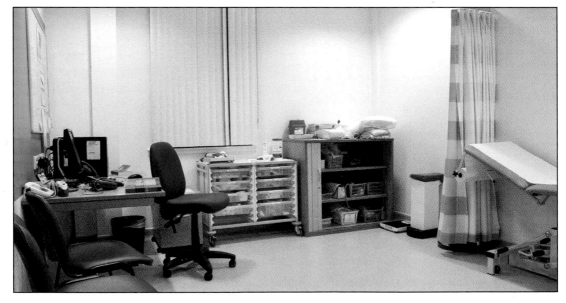

Doctor's room.

Fiona showed them where the medicine was kept. Inside a locked room there was a big cupboard, with separate organised compartments for all the different medicines. It was all extremely neat!

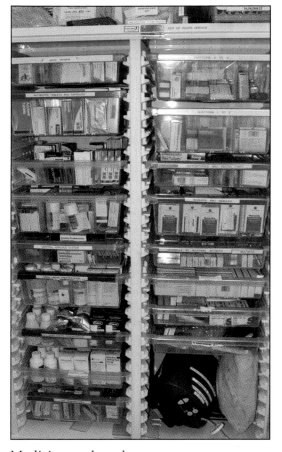

Medicine cupboard.

The doctor's medicine book, the 'BNF'.

"How do you remember all the different medicines?" asked Ava.

"We have a special book that we use as a reference. If we know what the illness is, we can use the book to look up the medicines that might be used to treat it. Medicines are updated all the time, so it is a very useful book, which I carry with me in my doctor's bag," explained Fiona.

Back in the doctor's room, there were other cupboards and shelves, storing all sorts of things like bandages, breathing devices, and various pieces of equipment used for a doctor's work.

Bandages and equipment stored neatly.   Patient's bed.

At the far side of the room was a bed for patients to lie on while they were checked by the doctor. On the wall was a poster of the human skeleton, which doctors used to help explain things to patients. There were also letters on a board used to check eyesight.

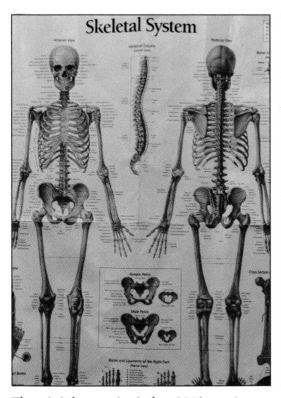

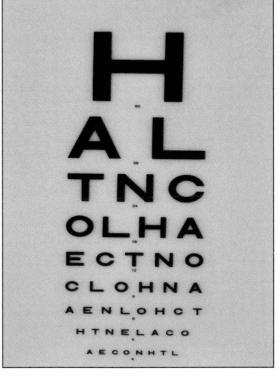

The adult human body has 206 bones!   Eyesight test.

"I'm going to show you two important pieces of equipment. Both are used for the heart. The first tool we have here is a **sphygmomanometer** [SFIG-moh-ma-NOM-i-ter]," she said.

The girls burst out laughing! "Sfygmom-what?" asked Ava, giggling. Fiona laughed too. "I told you we used long words! It's really not as complicated as it sounds, so don't be put off. You will be experts at this soon! We often call it *sphyg* [sfig] for short, which makes life a little easier, doesn't it?" she smiled.

"The sphyg machine measures the pressure of the blood. Blood pressure is the pressure made by the beating of your heart. The sphyg has a wide band that is wrapped around the top of your arm and air is pumped into the band to make it squeeze tightly," explained Fiona. "Doctors can find a lot of useful information about the health of your heart and your blood vessels

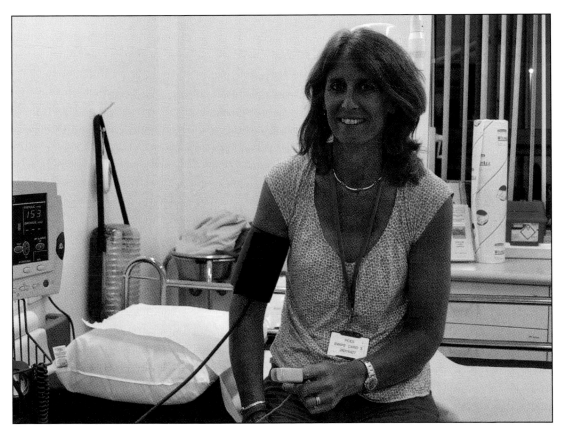

Fiona with the sphygmomanometer.

by taking the blood pressure. Maximum and minimum blood pressure are both measured. Now this is going to get a little complicated, so you need to concentrate!" she said.

"On our sphyg machine, we get two readings known as *systolic* and *diastolic* pressure. The *systolic* pressure is the maximum pressure in an artery at the moment when your heart is beating and pumping blood through your body. The *diastolic* pressure is the lowest pressure in an artery when your heart is resting, in between beats. Arteries are tube-shaped blood vessels that carry blood away from your heart, towards the rest of your body.

"Both the systolic and diastolic pressure measurements are important. If either one is high, it means you have high blood pressure, which is also called *hypertension*.

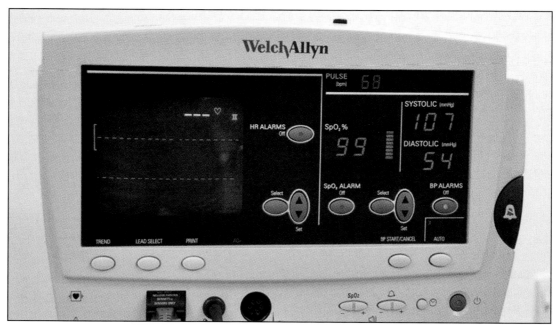

The results from the sphygmomanometer.

"You can see from the readings on the machine that the blood pressure shows a systolic - highest reading - of 107 on the top and diastolic - lowest reading - of 54 on the bottom. It also shows a pulse of 68 heart beats every minute," explained Fiona.

"One of our jobs as a doctor is to watch out for blood pressure that is either too high or too low, as it could mean that we have some problems," she said.

"The last thing I'm going to show you quickly is called a **defibrillator** [de-FIB-ril-lator]. This machine can mean the difference between life and death for people who are having a heart attack. If their heart stops, we use the defibrillator to basically 'jump start' their heart again," she explained.

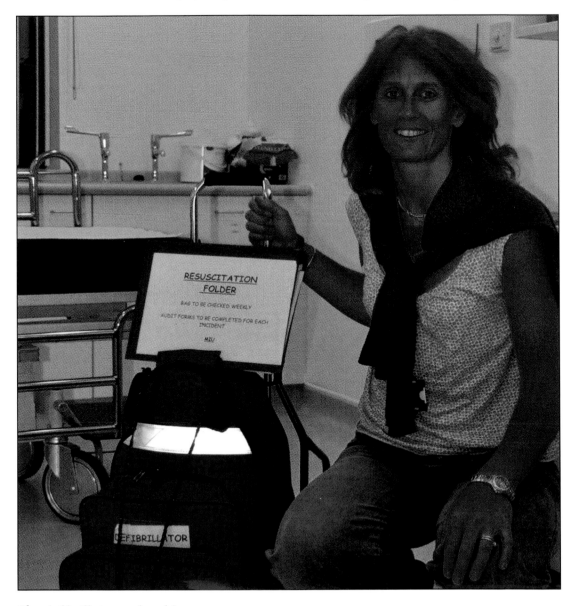

The defibrillator rucksack!

"What is your favourite part of being a doctor, Auntie Fee?" asked Skye.

"I love being a GP for many reasons," said Fiona. "The best part of the job is being able to help people feel better. It's a very rewarding job in that respect and is probably the main reason that people go into medicine.

"Being a family doctor means getting to know people, and this is one of the reasons I chose to be a GP, rather than work in the Accident and Emergency, or A&E section of the hospital. In A&E, people come and go in a rush, whereas being a GP in a village means that I get to know the families of Badaneel, and watch the children grow up.

"As a GP, you are also never bored!" she smiled. "There is always a challenge – every day is a new challenge, with different people, who have different things that need fixing. The medical profession is continuously finding new ways of treating people. As doctors, we are constantly learning every day.

"The other part of the job that I like is the flexibility. I've been a GP for a long time and when I was younger, I travelled the world and worked as a doctor in different countries. It was such a great experience. Being a GP means that you can work in different places.

"You can also choose the hours you work to an extent. For example, now that I have a family, I need to be at home to look after my children. As a GP, you can continue to work part-time to allow you to look after the family, as well as work. There are some jobs that have this flexibility, but many do not," she said.

"What is the worst part of your job?" asked Ava.

"The worst part is definitely seeing people who are sick and especially ones who are *terminally ill*. Terminally ill means that they will never get better.

"We can't cure them – all we can do is try to keep them as comfortable as possible for the remainder of their lives. It is always very sad seeing people ill, watching the families suffer, seeing sick children, or trying to persuade people to go to hospital when they don't want to go," said Fiona solemnly.

"What kind of illnesses do you see on a typical day?" asked Gracie.

"GPs see a very wide variety of illnesses, some of which are easy to cure and others that require specialist care. Some common areas that we deal with include:

- Children with a high temperature – this could mean they have a virus, ear infection, tonsillitis, chest infection or a range of other problems.
- Smoking-related problems – lung problems, shortness of breath.
- Asthma – this is a breathing illness, which we can usually manage.
- Heart problems.
- Contraception – helping women to stop getting pregnant.
- Headaches or migraines – helping people who suffer from very sore heads.
- Skin conditions – things like eczema or rashes.
- Muscular or joint problems, such as arthritis, which swells up your joints and makes them painful.
- Eyes, ears and throats.
- Hay fever and allergies.

"I also get lots of nice things to deal with like smelly feet, bottom problems, snotters, dandruff, body odour, and many other things that people don't like to talk about!" she smiled.

"Ewww, yuk!" said Gracie, grimacing.

Fiona laughed. "It might sound disgusting, but when you are a doctor, it's really not too bad. We are used to dealing with all sorts of problems and it is our job to help people with any sort of illness. There is generally a medical explanation for a problem. For example, did you know that smelly feet are caused by bacteria? Bacteria love dark, damp places, like the inside of your shoes. When your feet sweat, the bacteria multiply in number. Under the right conditions, the bacteria grows by eating dead skin cells and oils from your skin. As they grow, they get rid of waste in the form of organic acids. It is the waste from the organic acids that smells bad!"

The Mackenzie girls were looking at Fee with their faces scrunched up! Fiona smiled. "Smelling things is actually a job," she said. "There are people who are employed as professional 'smellers'! Their job might involve smelling nice things like shampoos or new perfumes, but it can also be testing insoles used to prevent smelly feet or even underarm deodorants!"

Fiona at her desk.

"Why do people sweat?" asked Skye.

"Good question, Skye! It's actually a very clever system. Our normal body temperature is 37°C or 98.6°F. 'C' is short for degree Celsius and 'F' is short for degree Fahrenheit. They are both scales used to measure temperature. Most countries use Celsius, although some, like the United States, use Fahrenheit. The body likes being at normal temperature and if it gets too hot, the brain sends a message to tell the body to sweat, so that it can cool down. At this point, special glands in your body, called *sweat glands*, start making sweat. Sweat is very clever because it is mostly made of water, plus tiny amounts of other chemicals such as ammonia, urea, salts and sugars. The sweat leaves your skin through tiny holes called pores. When the sweat hits the air, it evaporates – this means it turns from a liquid into a vapour. As the sweat evaporates off your skin, you cool down. Pretty clever stuff isn't it? So, next time you are out on your bicycles on a hot, sunny day, you will know why you sweat!" she smiled.

The Mackenzie girls on their bicycles.

"Sweat is a great cooling system, but one thing to watch out for when you are playing is *dehydration* [de-hy-DRA-tion]," said Fiona. "Dehydration is a word used to describe what happens when there is not enough water in the body. The first sign of dehydration is thirst. Other symptoms might include dizziness, headaches, tiredness or dark coloured urine, which is the medical term for pee. When you sweat, you lose water so you need to drink more to top up the body's reserves and to stop you getting dehydrated."

"If sweat is made up of mostly water, then why does it smell?" asked Ava.

Fiona laughed. "Another good question!" she said. "It's a bit like the bacteria that we talked about on smelly feet. Sweat by itself doesn't smell at all. It's the bacteria that live on your skin that mix with the sweat and give it a stinky smell. When you reach puberty, special hormones affect the glands in your armpits — these glands make sweat that can really smell.

"Luckily, washing regularly with soap and water can usually keep stinky sweat under control. Many teenagers and adults also find that wearing deodorant helps. So don't worry about a little sweat — it's totally normal and everybody sweats. Sometimes too much sweating can be a sign that there is something wrong in the body, but this is rare in kids. If you notice more sweat, it's usually just a sign that it's time to start using a deodorant. But if you think you have a sweat problem, talk to your parents or your doctor about it."

"Do you work long hours, Auntie Fee," asked Skye.

"Most full-time GPs work at least forty-five hours per week. We can choose to work longer days, 8am to 6pm, which means that we can cover the forty-five hours in four and a half days.

"GPs can also choose to work extra hours as *locums* in another doctor's surgery. A locum is when we provide help in other villages, perhaps when

the local doctor is not available. In addition, doctors also work *on call*, which means that you can be at home, but you must be available to receive a call to go and help a patient.

"I work for two and a half days per week. By cramming as much work as possible into these days, I have the rest of the week free to spend time with your cousins and look after the family. It's a very flexible system, where you get paid for the amount of work that you do," she explained.

"Doctors have a lot of responsibility, but we are well paid. It is a very good job and a very rewarding one."

Fiona on the phone.

"How do you become a doctor?" asked Skye.

"Firstly, and very importantly, you need to enjoy working with people and have a commitment to helping them," said Fiona. "There are many other jobs in the medical profession that don't involve as much human contact, but a GP requires a great deal!" she smiled.

"Becoming a doctor is not an easy option; it takes years of study and hard work. To begin with, you must study extremely hard at school so that you have the top grades needed to get into medical school.

"After you have got top marks at school and done well at university, you must also work alongside experienced people to learn the job properly.

"In addition to this, if you would like to become a specialist, you need to study more to become an expert. There are at least sixty different specialist doctors, along with many complicated names! For example:

- Paediatrics [pee-de-AT-rics] – children's doctors.
- Gynaecology [guy-na-COL-o-gy] – doctors who specialise in women's health.
- Surgery – operations on various parts of the body.
- Orthopaedics [or-tho-PEE-dics] – doctors who look after the muscles and skeletons in the body.
- Ophthalmology [op-thal-MOL-o-gy] – doctors who look after the eyes.

"Phew!" said Fiona. "It sounds like an awful lot when you put it like that. Being a doctor requires a great deal of training but, like any work, it doesn't feel like work if you enjoy it," she smiled.

Fiona the doctor at work.

"Once you have done all that, are you finished with studying?" asked Skye.

"Well, yes and no!" laughed Fiona. "In life, we never stop learning, or at least we shouldn't! As doctors we need to keep learning about new medicines and different ways to help patients get better.

"Many of my friends are also doctors, and we have a meeting every month to share experiences and learn from each other. Each time we meet, someone has to present a different topic – it could be anything from updates on the latest way to deal with heart attacks, to ways of treating people with allergies. Every week is completely different. To make it more fun, we have a cake competition, so each week we have a new cake to enjoy while we have our chat. I can assure you, some of the cakes are delicious. I imagine you girls don't like cake?" she laughed.

"Yes!" screamed the Mackenzie girls, nearly blowing off Fiona's ears. "We love cake!" they cried.

"Well, maybe if you become a doctor, you will be able to have special meetings with cake!" she laughed. "There are many good reasons to become a doctor, but did you know that we also have our own *Doctor, Doctor* jokes?"

The Mackenzie girls shook their heads. "No," they replied curiously. "We like jokes though," said Ava, smiling cheekily.

"Well," said Fiona, "*Doctor, Doctor* jokes are very old. Some say that people have been telling *Doctor, Doctor* jokes since Ancient Roman times, which is a very long time ago!" she laughed. "Here are some I have heard recently:

"Doctor, doctor, I can't get to sleep.
Lie on the edge of the bed and you'll soon drop off!"

The Mackenzie girls giggled. "That's quite funny!" said Ava as Fiona continued:

"Doctor, doctor, I feel like a carrot.
Don't get yourself in a stew.

"Doctor, doctor I feel like a sheep.
Oh that's very baaaaaaaad!

"Doctor, doctor, I feel like a pair of curtains.
Pull yourself together, man.

"Doctor, doctor - I've got a little bit of lettuce sticking out of my bottom.
I'm afraid it's just the tip of the iceberg!"

The girls were in fits of giggles and particularly liked the bottom joke – a joke about a bottom was *always* funny.

"Okay," said Fiona, still laughing, "I'd better get to work. Do you understand more about what doctors do now?" she asked.

"Oh yes," replied the girls. "It's a lot of work but if you enjoy being a doctor, then it doesn't feel like work. You get to help people all the time, which makes you feel happy. You also get paid well and have flexible working hours, which helps you manage work and family at the same time," said Gracie.

"That's right!" said Fiona. "Now I had better head off to see if I can help anyone today. See you soon, girls!" she called as the Mackenzie girls headed home with Mother.

It had been another very interesting day! The Mackenzie girls thought that being a doctor sounded like a good job, but one thing was for sure – if they wanted to be a doctor they were going to have to do a lot of extra homework and study very hard! They decided to think about it for a while, and hopefully learn about some other jobs. Ava, Skye and Gracie hadn't yet decided what they wanted to do when they grew up, but they had learnt a great deal about what other people do all day!

"Can we go and play now, Mama?" asked Gracie with her best smile. "I'm afraid not, Gracie," said Mother. "You are very nearly finished with the work you started this morning and do you know what one of the most important lessons of working is?"

The girls shook their head. "Do a good job?" asked Gracie. "Absolutely," said Mother, "and do you know one of the most important things about doing a good job?" The girls shook their heads again.

"*Finish* the job," smiled Mother. "One of the most important things is to finish a job. If Auntie Fee didn't finish her job, people could die. I know that finishing the weeding is not as important as finishing a doctor's job, but it is a good habit to get into. You have nearly completed the back path, so why don't you all go and finish that? Then you can play."

Whilst the girls were not overly pleased, they didn't mind too much. The sun was shining, they had spent an amazing morning doughnuting and jumping in the sea, they had learnt all about being a doctor, and there was still plenty time left to play, if they hurried up!

The end.

What do the grown-ups do?

The books are available in paperback through all good bookstores as well as through www.troubador.com and other places online. For more information, please check the website **www.kidseducationalbooks.com**.

The What do the grown-ups do? series in order of publication:

Book 1: Joe the Fisherman

Book 2: Papa the Stockfarmer

Book 3: Sean the Actor

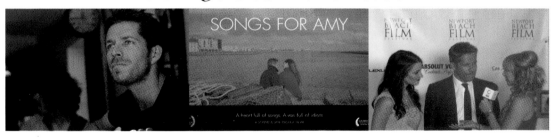

Book 4: Fiona the Doctor

Book 5: Richard the Vet

Book 6: Gordon the Wildlife Filmmaker

More coming soon!